Little Pearl

GW00726127

Book 1

Little Pearl

By Helen Haraldsen

Little Pearl

Copyright © 2019 to Helen Haraldsen

www.helenharaldsen.co.uk

All rights reserved. Apart from short quotations within critical pieces and reviews, no part of this book may be used or reproduced in any manner (including scanning, uploading and electronic sharing) without written permission by the author. Doing so without permission is considered unlawful piracy, and theft of the author's intellectual property.

This book is a work of fiction based on the author's life. Any resemblance to any other persons, living or dead, is purely coincidental.

Cover design, editing and formatting by Let's Get Booked:

www.letsgetbooked.com

Print ISBN: 978-1-9160112-3-6

eBook ISBN: 978-1-9160112-4-3

Third edition with minor changes

Contents

Author's Note

*"Remember me when you ride those 17hh warmbloods
and sports horses. Remember me when you are grown
and competing in earnest. I may not be the fanciest horse
you will ever ride, but I was the best horse I could be
when you needed me. Remember me."*

~ The first pony's plea, author unknown

Little Pearl (aged 14) and Helen in 1992

This book was written in memory of Little Pearl, my first pony, and to recognise all the other first horses and ponies out there. Those wonderful animals that are quiet, safe and forgiving enough to be our firsts deserve a very special place in our hearts. They put up with the mistakes we make through lack of experience and knowledge and help us to learn. We owe them so much and must always appreciate and honour them.

I have very fond memories of Pearl. She was a stubborn wotsit and had very firm ideas about what she thought was worth doing and what was a waste of time, but she was a good teacher and taught me a lot about *a lot*. Pearl never did anything unless she could see a good reason for it and, like Amber, at first, I felt out of place at shows with the other riders on 'proper' show ponies.

I soon learnt, however, that a pony's value is not really measured by how high it can jump or how fast it can go. A pony's value is measured by the trust placed in it by its rider, by the bond of unspoken communication they share, the feeling of oneness and complete confidence in each other. I was lucky enough to experience this wonderful relationship with Pearl and I will never forget what she gave me.

She wasn't the fastest or the boldest, but she took care of me and became my best friend.

Our ponies are always trying to tell us something if we would only listen. If I had listened sooner, I would have heard Pearl say, "Don't worry. I'll look after you."

Always listen. You don't know what you could be missing.

Little Pearl (aged 27) and Helen in 2005

For my parents who bought Little Pearl for me and started me on the path towards sharing my life with the most wonderful friends anyone could wish for –

THE HORSES

– One –

Make Believe

"Are you ready Dad? Hurry up or we'll be late!"

"I can't find the car keys!" called the harassed voice of Mr Anderson from the kitchen, where he could be heard rummaging through coat pockets and searching under newspapers and piles of junk mail for the missing keys. Amber flicked her long blonde plait back over her shoulder and checked her watch impatiently. If he didn't find them soon, they would be late for their ride.

Amber Anderson was eleven years old and an only child. She lived with her parents and her pet dog and cat – plus the goldfish Freddy and Felix. The whole family were animal mad, but horses were everyone's favourite. Amber couldn't remember a time when she hadn't been passionate about horses. When she was in infant school, she recalled painting crude pictures of a blob with four legs and proudly telling the teacher it was her pony. She didn't have a pony though, except for the one in her imagination, which wasn't that bad because an imaginary pony can be a perfect pony.

Her imaginary pony had been a gleaming grey mare called Sapphire, inspired by pictures she had seen in a book about Pegasus. They always won show jumping competitions in Amber's garden, where she pretended she was riding to glory against a field of famous competitors she'd seen jumping huge fences at Hickstead and Olympia. What's more, her imaginary pony didn't need to be groomed, mucked out or ridden on cold, rainy days. But even though Sapphire was the perfect pony and provided her with hours of daydreaming fun, Amber always longed for the real thing.

Eventually, on her tenth birthday, her parents decided to grant her wish. The memory of that day still made her smile. She had come down to breakfast in her pyjamas to find her parents sitting at the kitchen table, looking at her over the top of a mound of presents. Often, presents can be more exciting when they are wrapped up than when the contents are revealed, but not these presents. She tore the wrapping off the first gift to reveal a deep blue sweatshirt with a pretty palomino pony emblazoned on the front. The next parcel held a pair of jodhpurs. Amber had started to feel a swell of excitement as she continued unwrapping presents to find a hat covered in a brightly coloured silk, a pair of gloves and some shiny black riding boots. Alight with happiness she had looked hopefully at her parents.

"Your last present couldn't be wrapped," her mother explained. "We've booked you a course of five group and five individual riding lessons at a riding school half an hour from here." She paused to smile at Amber's glowing face. "You'd better get dressed. Your first one is today."

***

Pine Tree Riding School was set out in the countryside amidst the fells and forestry. As soon as she stepped out of the car and smelled the intoxicating aroma of sweet hay, leather, and horse, Amber knew she was going to love it there. She felt as if she had returned to some long-lost favourite place she hadn't been to for a long time.

Claire – the owner and instructor – led a small, grey pony that reminded her of Sapphire into the yard. He was called Blaze, and according to Claire, was "a nice schoolmaster."

Amber hadn't heard the term 'schoolmaster' before, so Claire explained that the word is used to describe safe, experienced ponies. Amber could only think of old-fashioned school teachers she had seen on TV who threw board rubbers at naughty children or gave them the cane. She was a bit worried about Blaze 'The Schoolmaster'. *"What if I do something wrong?"* she thought. *"Will he buck me off to teach me a lesson?"*

Amber needn't have worried. After being shown how to mount and hold the reins properly, a stable girl led her into an outdoor arena where three other children were waiting on ponies. Next to each pony was a helper who had the pony on a lead rein just like Blaze. Claire explained how to use their legs and hands to encourage the ponies to move forward, change direction and stop.

Amber felt extremely precarious on Blaze's back. He was only twelve hands high, but she felt a long way from the ground. She was glad she had someone there to help her while she got used to the sensation of Blaze's body swaying underneath her as he walked. It was a strange feeling; powerful and helpless at the same time. Amber marvelled at the way Blaze turned when she asked him. She could get him to stop from a very gentle squeeze on the reins and move forward with a little wiggle of her legs. He was very responsive, and she knew that he was reacting to her commands rather than the helper who was really only there for support and encouragement.

Gradually, as the riders became more confident, the helpers unclipped the lead ropes and let them carry on by themselves. Amber was delighted that she managed to get Blaze to walk in a figure of eight all by herself. She became lost in the moment. It was just her and Blaze working together. Amber was so focussed on communicating with the pony, she forgot about everything and everyone else. All too soon the lesson was over, but Amber knew she was hooked.

"I hope you enjoyed it everyone," Claire said cheerfully. She was answered with four nodding heads and lots of "yeah, great," and "brilliant," from the young riders.

"Good," she replied, "next time you'll be having a go at trotting."

Amber had enjoyed her lessons on Blaze, and when she had had all ten, Claire thought she was competent enough to go for a hack out.

Amber enjoyed hacking out much more than the lessons. It was lovely riding through the forest, breathing in the smell of fresh pine, or being blasted by invigorating winds on the open fells. As time went by and she became more experienced, she was able to try different ponies and enjoy canters and gallops with the others, instead of having to go on ahead with the ride leader while the others cantered up behind.

On seeing her joy after every hack, her parents, who had both ridden when they were young, decided to join her every Sunday.

***

"I've found them!" Mr Anderson cheered, running from the kitchen clutching the elusive keys tightly in one hand, as if he feared they might escape and get lost again. "Let's go."

Amber rolled her eyes and chuckled as they dashed down the drive to the car.

"We'll be just in time." She thought to herself, fastening the seatbelt across her chest.

"I wonder who I'll be riding. I know who I want it to be."

With that the car rolled onto the road, heading in the direction of Pine Tree Riding School.

– Two –

Pearl

"Phew! Just in time," Amber sighed in relief. They had arrived at the stables just as the horses and ponies were being led out into the yard, while riders stood around waiting to find out who they were riding. Amber spotted Claire, who was leading a piebald cob out of the barn, and ran straight to her. Claire saw her coming and gave her a knowing smile.

"I know who you're after," she said.

"*Please*," Amber pleaded, her hands meeting in prayer.

"Oh alright, but you really should try other ponies you know. It will help you to improve as a rider."

Amber shrugged, "I know, but I just love her."

"I don't know what it is about that pony that's got you so smitten. No-one else ever asks for her." Claire shook her head and stroked the piebald's nose. "Lisa is holding her and Polly over by the water trough. Tell your dad he can ride Polly today."

Amber told her dad what Claire had said, and they walked together to where Lisa was standing with the ponies. Pine Tree had sixteen horses and ponies; mostly natives and cobs, as they were hardy, sensible and able to carry riders of all shapes and sizes.

Ever since the first time she'd ridden her, Amber's favourite was a black Fell x Welsh pony called Pearl. She was a little under 13 hands high, with a long, flowing mane and tail. Amber adored Pearl's cheeky face and the mischievous eyes that peeped out from under her long forelock. Whenever Amber rode Pearl, the two seemed to click. She didn't understand why, but they seemed to have a special bond that she hadn't felt with the other ponies.

It was a blustery day. The ponies' manes whipped about, and sharp blasts of cold air caused Amber's eyes to water. They walked in single file up to the gate before entering the forest. Tall pine trees stood in neat rows like silent sentinels, guarding the paths and keeping the forest's secrets. As soon as the ponies' feet touched the soft dirt track, they were on their toes, champing on the bits. Amber noticed that her dad had to work hard to keep Polly under control as she side-stepped and tossed her head, trying to get free of his grip on the reins. Polly was a pure Fell pony. She was short legged and stocky but incredibly strong and fast, with amazing stamina. Claire only let experienced riders on Polly. Amber patted Pearl, who was always steady and safe and felt glad she was riding her and not getting her shoulders yanked out of their sockets.

By the time the ride was over and they traipsed back into the yard, Amber's face was numb with cold and spattered with mud from being at the back of the galloping horses. She ran her stirrups up and led Pearl into her stall in the barn. She took off Pearl's saddle and bridle and gave her a good brush all over to remove the sweat and dirt.

"Good girl," she whispered as she brushed. "I hope Claire lets me ride you next week. I don't want to ride any of the others. You're the best, aren't you girl?"

Pearl gave her a little nudge as if to say, "I agree."

Amber dug deep into her pocket and pulled out a carrot she had brought for her favourite companion.

As she closed the stall door behind her, Amber wished for the week to pass quickly so that she could be back riding Pearl again.

***

The following Saturday morning Amber dragged herself out of bed and pulled on her jeans and her favourite green t-shirt, grumpy at the thought of having to go shopping with her mum. She trudged down the stairs and into the kitchen.

Mrs Anderson looked up from the book she was reading and said nonchalantly, "You'll have to get changed dear. You can't go in those good clothes."

"What?" Said Amber, creasing her brow in confusion, "I'm not going to go shopping in my old clothes, am I? I'd look a right sight."

"Ah, but we're not going shopping today," her mother replied, closing her book and standing up, "we're going for a little surprise. Put on your riding clothes."

Amber didn't need telling twice. She'd much rather go riding than shopping any day, but they'd never been on a Saturday before. Wondering what was going on, she changed into her jodhpurs and flew down the stairs, where her parents were both waiting by the door, whispering to each other. As soon as Amber appeared, they abruptly stopped and smiled warmly at her.

"Ready love?" her dad asked. She nodded and followed them out to the car.

"Where are we going?" Amber asked, although she thought she already knew the answer.

"You'll see," replied her mum, tapping her nose with a finger. "Like I said, it's a surprise."

"Well it's obviously a surprise involving ponies," thought Amber to herself, *"and anything to do with ponies is ok with me."*

She settled back in the car watching houses and other cars whiz by in a haze of colour, while butterflies formed in her tummy, tickling her with their delicate wings making her feel both nervous and excited. Oh, what was the surprise going to be? She couldn't wait to find out.

- Three -

⚘

Surprise

Finally, they pulled into Pine Tree's car park. Walking into the barn, Amber could see there were only two ponies in the stalls. One was Pearl, and the other was a Fell pony called Honey that her mother liked to ride. This had happened before. One time, her dad had brought her to the stables on a Monday during a school holiday. That was strange as Monday was the ponies' day off – when they all got a day's relaxation in the fields. But on that Monday, there had been two ponies in the barn and Amber had been worried, wondering why things were different. Mr Anderson had laughed and told her that the other horses and ponies were out in the fields, but he had hired two so they could go out together on their own. It had been great, just the two of them; they'd been able to decide when to trot or canter and could choose where to go instead of having to follow the ride leader. It looked like he'd done the same thing again, but she was wondering why he'd only hired two ponies when all three of them were there.

"Who are you going to ride, Dad?" she asked.

Mr and Mrs Anderson exchanged a knowing look before Mr Anderson answered.

"Well, actually, we haven't hired them... we've *bought* them. Pearl is for you and Honey is for Mum and me so that we can take turns to ride out with you."

Amber didn't quite know what to feel, say or do after that bombshell. She blinked hard, feeling positively queasy. *"Pearl is mine? Pearl is my pony? Is this a dream?"* She couldn't believe it.

"But...it's not even my birthday," she exclaimed weakly, leaning against the wall as if she needed its support to stop her from toppling to the ground.

"Oh, well if you want to wait until your birthday we can tell Claire–"

"*NO!* Of course I don't want to wait," Amber interrupted her mother, "I definitely want her now! Thank you, thank you, thank you. It's just such a surprise and so unexpected and for no reason and…" She had to stop to get her breath back.

"We just thought the time was right. You've proved you're serious by not chickening out on cold, wet days, and it's a good, healthy hobby we can all enjoy," her mum explained.

The three of them stood looking at the ponies – who were happily munching on their hay, completely oblivious to three people standing staring at them – while the idea that they owned these beautiful animals sunk in. After a few moments of thoughtful silence, Mrs Anderson suggested that Amber should go and say hello to her new pony. Amber snapped out of her reverie and practically skipped over to Pearl's stall, marvelling at the fact that she hadn't thought of doing so herself.

A thought suddenly occurred to Amber while she lovingly pulled her fingers through Pearl's long mane, gently easing out tangles and pieces of hay.

"Where are we going to keep them, Dad?" she asked, "Here?"

Mr Anderson, who had been looking at Honey with his wife, came over to Pearl's stall.

"No, not here love. There's a farm just up the road. The farmer's daughter has a horse, and he's agreed to let us have DIY livery. It'll mean we have to come through every day after school to see to them."

"That's okay," Amber replied brightly, "Maybe I'll be able to make friends with the farmer's daughter, and she could come for rides with us."

Her father chuckled, "Maybe dear, but I think it's unlikely. The farmer's daughter is twenty-three, and her horse is a 16.2hh Irish Draught. These two of ours could practically walk under its tummy."

"Oh," said Amber, slightly crestfallen. "Well, never mind."

***

That night Amber's sleep was brimming with dreams. As her mind sifted and sorted through the day's information, storing it as life-long memories, she relived

16

everything that had happened; from arriving at the farm to meeting Jerry the farmer and turning the ponies out into their new field. When her alarm clock went off, she was smiling in her sleep, leaning on the field gate watching the ponies grazing contentedly with the sun warming their coal black coats. She awoke with a start, feeling irritated that her wonderful dream had been disturbed. It took her a moment to remember that finally, her dream had become a reality. Happiness coursed through her like an electric current and made her feel wide awake. She dressed hurriedly and raced downstairs to see if anyone else was up yet.

***

Amber looked out of the window as they drove past Pine Tree. She could see the girls pushing wheelbarrows or carrying hay nets across the yard. It was strange to pass the car park and carry on up the bumpy track that led to the farm. As their car trundled into the farm yard, the front door of the house opened and a boy of about fourteen emerged, wearing green overalls and eating a slice of toast. He quickly climbed into a tractor and started it up. As he drove past them, he waved. He had the same friendly face, soft blue eyes and wide, smiling mouth as Jerry the farmer.

"He must be the farmer's son," thought Amber to herself, blushing as she waved back at him.

Two black and white collies bounded towards them, wagging their plumy tails and grinning broadly. Amber bent down and stroked their smiling faces. Amber's dog, a golden cocker spaniel called Kasper, viewed the farm dogs suspiciously. She was just about to speak to the dogs when a loud whistle pierced the air and they shot off after the retreating tractor like twin missiles. Kasper jumped and looked after them in surprise. His interest didn't last long though, as usual, and he soon had his nose to the ground again following all the interesting new smells.

With no more distractions, Amber and Mrs Anderson caught the ponies with ease and brought them in from the field.

After Mrs Anderson saddled Honey and Pearl, she checked that all the tack fitted comfortably, then they led the ponies into the yard and mounted. Amber buzzed with excitement. Although she had ridden Pearl many times, this was to be her first ride on her as her own pony.

She looked between Pearl's neat, pricked ears and felt her heart swell. She gave the pony a gentle nudge to walk on. Pearl didn't move a muscle except to sweep her ears back and lay them flat against her head. Amber looked at her mum, who seemed to be having the same trouble with Honey.

"What's wrong with them?" Amber moaned. "Why won't they go?"

"Because…" Mrs Anderson puffed, "neither of these two are used to leading. They're so used to following other horses they don't know how to think for themselves." She dismounted and took the reins over Honey's head. "We're going to have to show them what we want them to do."

With that, she began to lead Honey down the track. As soon as Pearl saw another pony in front of her that she could follow, she flicked her ears forward and sauntered after it as if nothing had happened.

Amber got the feeling that owning a pony would be a little harder than she first thought.

- Four -

An Unexpected Meeting

It had taken them several weeks to be able to get out for a decent ride. Neither pony was willing to lead, nor would they walk side by side. One was always trying to slip in and hide behind the other.

"We must teach them to think for themselves," became Mrs Anderson's motto. "They've got to stop being so dependent on each other."

At first, the rides were terribly hard work. The ponies would stop regularly and refuse to walk past any rock, gate or dandelion for fear that some great monster was lurking behind it, waiting to pounce on them. There was lots of dismounting and dragging as well as sitting, patiently waiting for the stubbornness to pass and for the ponies to give in. They would never let the ponies turn around when they tried or allow them to hide behind each other. Riding out became more of a battle than a pleasure and progress was painfully slow. Amber began to wonder if she had imagined the bond she had with Pearl as the pony tested her patience to the limit.

"This is ridiculous," she whined one day when both ponies had planted themselves at the end of the farm lane and refused to turn right towards the forestry, trying instead to turn left and head back to their former home at Pine Tree.

"They're not getting any better." Amber pulled on her right rein to try and encourage Pearl to turn in the direction they wanted to go, but the pony was having none of it. She shook her head but didn't move. If Pearl couldn't go where she wanted, she wasn't going anywhere at all.

"We have to stick at it and persevere." Mrs Anderson puffed, allowing herself a short rest from encouraging Honey to move forward. "If we are firm and consistent, we will get through to them…at some point."

Eventually, after lots of hard work, Honey and Pearl became a little more confident and would walk alongside each other without seeing monsters in every hedgerow, though Honey still wouldn't put her head past Pearl's shoulder. She remained too nervous to take the lead.

The experience had helped Amber immensely. She had grown into a stronger rider in her battles with Pearl, and she had learnt the art of quiet perseverance, of insisting on obedience and cooperation without losing her temper or using violence. Now, when she asked Pearl to do something, there was no resistance. They were a team who respected each other and could face anything together. It felt good.

***

One day Amber and her mother decided on a ride through the forest. The two ambled along silently, enjoying the cold, fresh air.

Suddenly, they heard the pounding of hooves and a shrill, "look out!" from behind them. Before they had time to turn and see what the fuss was about, a small pony thundered past. It was ridden by a young girl who was frantically tearing at her reins trying to stop her pony's headlong gallop. She disappeared around the corner in a cloud of dust, and the rapid hoof beats receded. Amber and Mrs Anderson exchanged looks of surprise and the ponies snorted to show their displeasure at the sudden shock of the disturbance.

"Phew. I wonder who that was?" Amber exclaimed. "Her pony looked like a *maniac*."

"Yes," agreed Mrs Anderson, "and it looks like she's out on her own. I wouldn't be happy about you riding a loony like that at all, never mind on your own."

They hadn't gone much further when they heard hoof beats again, this time coming towards them. It was the same girl that had just charged past. She trotted back to join them, her chestnut pony tossing its head, and curling its upper lip to reveal long, yellow teeth.

"Hi," the girl said cheerfully. She looked about Amber's age, but she was taller with long legs that hung well below her pony's sides. "I just came back to say sorry for charging past you like that. I didn't mean to, but Flash had taken off and when he goes – I can't stop him, he's so str–"

The last word was lost as Flash snatched the reins and jumped forward, nearly dragging his rider over his head. She quickly recovered and reined him in as he continued to bob about restlessly.

"Sorry," she said.

"He seems a bit of a handful," observed Mrs Anderson, eyeing Flash disdainfully.

"Yes," agreed the girl brightly as she was pulled forward again, "he's a total nutter."

"Don't your parents mind you riding out on such a...er...*lively* pony?" Mrs Anderson chose her words carefully.

"Oh no," the girl replied, "I've been riding since I was three," she beamed with pride.

"Oh," said Mrs Anderson, simply. She didn't think having ridden since the age of three was enough to mean the girl was safe on this pony, but she decided to change the subject.

"Well, this is Amber," she said, indicating her daughter, "and I'm Carol, Amber's mum. We've not had our ponies long. They're kept at Shaw Farm in the village."

"I'm Joanne, and I live on the track just before the farm. You'll ride past my house."

"Oh yes," piped Amber, "we saw the stables and wondered who lived there. We've never seen you about before."

"Well, I don't hack out much," explained Joanne. "I practice jumping in the field most of the time. Obviously they've been too wet to ride on over winter, so we've just gone to a few indoor jumping competitions and Flash has had a bit of a rest. I've got to start doing something with him now though to get him fit again."

Amber thought Flash looked fit enough. He was revving himself up again, grabbing the reins and threatening to leap forward.

"I'll have to go now. The big hill is coming up and Flash will take off again. Maybe we could ride out together sometime? I don't do it much 'cause there's no-one to go with. It would be better to have some company." Joanne just about got her sentence finished before their track reached the bottom of the forestry hill. Flash gave a mighty fly buck and launched himself into the air as if he was clearing an imaginary jump. He used the force of the leap to propel himself into a powerful gallop and was away up the hill like a streak of lightning, his hoofbeats reverberating through the valley.

Honey and Pearl tossed their heads and quickened their step, but made no attempt to go after him.

"Well, there's one thing for certain," said Mrs Anderson, "if Joanne wants to ride with us, she'll have to learn to slow that lunatic down. These two will never keep up with him."

- Five -

An Unusual Invitation

After their brief meeting, whenever the Andersons drove past Joanne's house on their way to the farm, Amber would call in and ask if she was riding with them. At first, they didn't get to talk with Joanne much as she was always fighting to hang on to Flash as he jogged, snatched, bucked and leapt, or galloped off, leaving them behind.

Flash would wind himself up like a tightly coiled spring until eventually he would just explode from walk into a flat-out gallop. There was nothing Joanne could do to stop him except wait until he decided he wanted to be stopped, and then she would trot back and re-join them until the next time. Amber couldn't believe how Flash could go from nothing to full-speed in the blink of an eye. She decided that Joanne's pony could be compared to a Ferrari, while Honey and Pearl were more like Ford Fiestas.

Gradually, after a number of hair-raising rides for Joanne, Flash began to calm down slightly. He would still champ on his bit and toss his head around, and when they started to trot, he would crab step sideways and get upset because he couldn't keep up with the Fell ponies' smart trotting pace. But the bolting eventually decreased until it stopped almost completely. After a couple of weeks of being exposed to the Fells' calming influence, he finally managed to walk up the forestry hill.

"It's much better now Flash doesn't take off all the time, isn't it?" remarked Amber as she and Joanne were out on their own one day, and finally able to have a conversation.

"He's probably just worked out that there's no point rushing 'cause your ponies are so slow," Joanne laughed.

Amber wasn't sure if she was joking or if she was having a subtle dig at the Fellies. She scrutinised Joanne's face for clues to reveal what she was thinking, but Joanne quickly changed the subject.

"The season will be starting soon," she said, "I can't wait. I really want to do well this year as it will be my last year on Flash."

Amber was puzzled, "What's the season?" she asked, "And what do you mean, it's your last year on Flash?"

Joanne explained that 'the season' referred to the season of outdoor competitions which started on Easter Monday and finished at the end of September.

"I'm getting taller, and soon I'll be too big to ride him. I'll need a 14.2hh next year," she beamed, excited at the thought of a new pony.

"What will happen to Flash then?" Asked Amber, feeling quite alarmed. She had never thought of 'growing out' of a pony like you do with clothes and shoes. After all, her dad wasn't short, and he rode Honey, who was nearly 14hh, without looking particularly under-horsed.

"Oh, he'll go to Matthew, so he can start competing properly. He'll never win anything on Sam."

Matthew was Joanne's eight-year-old brother. Amber had seen him in the yard sitting on a bucket, looking gloomy while his mother brushed a small, hairy bay cob-type pony. She couldn't imagine Matthew riding Flash in a million years.

"What sort of things do you do at shows?" Amber enquired.

"Oh, there's all sorts," Joanne replied enthusiastically. "There's gymkhanas where you can do show jumping, games and handy pony…oh, and equitation if you want. Then there's hunter trials, horse trials, tetrathlons, camp and Member's Cup. I like hunter trials best."

Amber's head was reeling. *What on earth was a 'handy pony'? What's equitation and what was it… trakalons?*

She asked Joanne, who then went into tremendous detail describing the difference between show jumping and cross-country, what Pony Club games were and what you did at Member's Cup.

"I just tend to do jumping and games. I only do dressage at Member's Cup 'cause you have to. It's so boring, trotting around in circles, and Flash is useless at it – he usually ends up jumping out of the arena."

"Er…what's dressage?" Asked Amber, whose head continued to swim with information.

"It's supposed to be a test of the horse's obedience to the rider," sighed Joanne, sounding suddenly bored, "and you have to plait up and learn a sequence of movements that you remember and perform inside a rectangle on the ground. It's dead boring, so I don't do it."

Amber was just about to ask why it was boring to have an obedient pony, when Joanne had an idea and exclaimed, "Hey, we'll be putting our jumps out soon now the fields are drying up again. Why don't you come and have a go?"

"Yeah…sure," Amber agreed politely, but inside she felt nervous. She'd never jumped before and didn't know the first thing about it.

And neither did Pearl.

- Six -

Jumping

Amber had had an awful day at school. First, she hadn't brought her science homework in because she couldn't find it. Stig had been asleep on top of it and she hadn't thought to look under the cat.

Stig was so called because a lady had found him and another young kitten inside a cardboard box on a rubbish dump. She had heard them mewing and opened the box to investigate. One of the kittens was a small tabby female that she decided to keep for herself. The other kitten was a black and white male, and the lady – although desperately sorry for both of them – knew she could only keep one. She had taken the male kitten into the Post Office where Mrs Anderson had worked at the time and asked if anyone was interested in him. Mrs Anderson took

32

one look at the tiny, helpless creature and agreed to take him there and then. When she brought him home and explained the situation, there had only been one name for him: Stig, after the book, *Stig of the Dump*, as Carol Anderson was a bit of a bookworm.

That tiny, half-starved kitten had grown into a large, sleek adult cat. He was now so enormous that it was quite possible for him to lie on a sheet of paper and completely hide it from view.

After getting in trouble for her lack of homework, her mind was too busy fretting about it to concentrate during the mental maths test, and she'd only got 9 out of 15. To top it all off, Miss Burton had given them maths homework.

Maths was Amber's most dreaded lesson, and she was quite convinced that she was subjected to enough of it at school without having to do it at home as well. Teachers were evil, she decided.

Now that home time was approaching, the knot that had been growing inside her all day began to twist and coil, feeling like it was both crushing and tickling her insides at the same time. In less than two hours she would be having her first attempt at jumping in front of her parents and Joanne, and probably Joanne's parents too. Amber clutched her stomach as a sudden wave of nausea washed over her.

***

At the farm she brushed Pearl half-heartedly as the knot in her stomach continued to tighten. Mr Anderson had brought her a sandwich as usual, to keep her hunger at bay until tea-time, but she had been unable to eat it, feeling that the knot had extended to her throat.

Mrs Anderson laughed at her daughter, "Amber, you look white. You don't have to do this you know, nobody's forcing you." She placed a reassuring hand on her daughter's shoulder.

But Amber felt that she did have to do it. She didn't want Joanne thinking she was afraid, and her new friend's remark about the Fell ponies being slow still rankled her. She wanted to prove that Pearl could jump. And so, with grim determination, she saddled up, mounted, and rode down the lane to Joanne's house.

Flash and Sam were tied outside the stables. Joanne was fiddling with Flash's bridle which jingled and jangled like Santa's sleigh, while her mum was extracting twigs and leaves from Sam's bushy black mane. Joanne's curly-haired brother Matthew sat on a low wall examining an ant that was scurrying across his hand. He and Sam seemed to be a well-matched pair, as they both looked rather shaggy and a bit grubby. Joanne noticed Mrs Anderson opening the gate into the yard and ran over to greet them.

"Hi," she called out cheerfully. "We're nearly ready. Mum's just finishing de-tangling Sam."

She pointed to a small gate beyond the stables. "The jumps are just in there. Go in and warm-up. We won't be a minute."

On the other side of the gate was a small paddock; 'the jumping field' as Joanne called it. A number of jumps were spread around. Some were brightly coloured with white wings like those on TV, while others were made from old oil drums or lemonade crates.

Amber was quietly trotting Pearl around the perimeter of the field when Joanne and Matthew appeared through the gate. Flash practically exploded into the field despite all the straps and chains he had around his face and neck, while Sam plodded in sensibly behind.

Mrs Jones, Joanne's mum, introduced herself to Amber's parents and explained that her husband was at work. Then she addressed Joanne, who was explaining to Amber that Flash was wearing a martingale, grackle noseband, pelham and curb chain because he was even stronger at jumping than he was at hacking out.

"Right, Jo, take Flash round so Amber can see how it's done."

Joanne started to gather up her reins and Flash jumped as if he'd been electrocuted.

"And remember to take it *easy*. He isn't fully fit yet," Mrs Jones called out.

Flash side-stepped around the field in what Amber thought was supposed to be a trot, crunching his bit and foaming at the mouth. Then Joanne turned him towards a low cross pole.

Flash tossed his head back showing his wild white eyes. Then he rocked back on his haunches, grabbed the bit from Joanne's hands and raced madly towards the tiny jump.

When he got there, he devoured the jump in one massive stride then careered around the field for a few laps before he settled back to an uneasy, eye-rolling jog.

Amber looked at her parents, who appeared to be quite unnerved by Flash's unconventional approach to jumping. Mrs Jones had also noticed their worried expression.

"Perhaps Flash isn't the best example to watch," she offered. "He's much better over bigger jumps – he has to think about them, so it slows him down a bit. *You* go around Matthew and let Amber see how Sam does it."

Matthew flapped his short legs against Sam's sides and the pony walked obediently into the middle of the field. A little more leg flapping and they moved up to a steady trot.

Matthew trotted around the field a couple of times before giving a click with his tongue. Sam drifted easily into a slow, loping canter. As they came around the corner, Matthew pointed Sam at the same cross pole that

Joanne had jumped on Flash. As Sam saw the jump his ears pricked, but he did not increase his pace. Two strides out, Matthew gathered his reins and leant forward slightly as Sam picked up his feathery feet and hopped neatly over the jump. They cantered steadily away before coming back to a walk with just a gentle feel down the reins.

Amber couldn't believe how differently the two ponies approached jumping. She much preferred Sam's way; he was steady, but he looked as if he enjoyed himself. To her, it seemed that Flash didn't really like jumping. He approached a fence as if someone was chasing him with a cattle prod and he had to escape, whereas Sam looked completely happy.

Watching Sam, Amber relaxed, forgetting why she was there. Her stomach gave a sudden lurch as Mrs Jones' voice interrupted her thoughts.

"Well done Matthew. That was lovely. Now then Amber, how do you feel about having a go?"

– Seven –

The Green-Eyed Monster

That evening Amber put her homework and P.E kit into her bag ready for school the next day. Afterwards, she had a long bubble bath and got into bed with a *PONY* magazine, but she could not concentrate. The words blurred and swam in front of her eyes as her mind went back over the events of the day. She could still feel everyone's eyes on her following Mrs Jones' invitation to try Pearl over the jumps.

She decided to follow Matthew's example by allowing Pearl to trot around the field to warm-up. She used the time to try and remember all that Claire had taught her in her lessons; keep the hands still, shoulders back, head up, heels down, seat light, correct diagonal. But with five pairs of eyes following her every move, she began to get incredibly nervous. Eventually, after several laps around the field, Amber braced herself and turned Pearl around the corner towards the jump.

She clicked her tongue, sat down and put her leg on, but Pearl did not canter. In fact, she seemed to be slowing down. Someone shouted something that she didn't hear clearly but knew instinctively that it was 'kick on', or something similar. She kicked and tried to encourage Pearl verbally, but as they reached the point in front of the jump where they should have been taking off, Pearl ground to a halt and stopped dead in front of the poles. There was a moment's silence and Amber felt the heat in her cheeks, going redder still at the thought that everyone could see her humiliation.

"Not to worry dear," came Mrs Jones' buoyant voice. "Neither of you have done it before. Don't be put off by these two," she inclined her head back towards Matthew and Joanne. "They've been doing it for years. You just need to practice."

Mrs Jones patted Amber's leg. She gave Pearl – who hadn't budged from her position in front of the jump – a rub between the eyes and smoothed her forelock over the little white star on her face. Then she showed Amber how to shorten her stirrups for better balance and how to get into the jumping position.

"This is so you don't get left behind." She explained patiently. "When the horse jumps you have to follow the movement and allow her to stretch over the jump."

She mimed pushing her hands forward and her bottom out. Amber giggled at the sight of Mrs Jones squatting in the middle of the field, looking as if she were sitting on an invisible toilet simultaneously reading an invisible newspaper.

"Watch," she said, straightening up.

Matthew leapt over the little cross pole again to demonstrate the jumping position, and once more Sam popped over the jump and cantered away happily. Amber was instructed to follow on after Sam and let him give her a lead over the jump next time around.

She nudged Pearl with her heels and the pony grudgingly moved forward.

Sam sailed easily over the poles again, but despite Amber's best attempts, Pearl stopped dead in her tracks again. Hot tears stung Amber's eyes and her cheeks burned with the shame of failure.

Why was Pearl being so difficult? It was only a tiny, stupid, insignificant jump after all. It didn't even require her to make an effort. Amber knew Pearl was just being plain stubborn as she had shown on many occasions that if she didn't want to do something, then she wouldn't… not without a fight.

Amber was filled with a mixture of embarrassment, frustration and determination. Her nerves had gone, to be replaced with a fiery resolve that Pearl would get over the jump that evening, even if she had to wait until the stars came out.

It took four more attempts, the last with Mr Anderson running behind her, waving his arms and shouting various unpleasant words at Pearl before she resigned herself to the fact that she was going to have to go over this obstacle in front of her one way or another.

At first it looked as if she was going to stick with her preferred option of refusing the jump. Amber felt her heart drop, but although she was exhausted, she summoned a growl from the pit of her stomach and so, on the sixth attempt, Pearl decided it might be easier to simply go over it.

Everyone was so pleased and fed up in equal measures that they all cheered loudly when Pearl landed over her first jump. Amber's embarrassment was replaced by a surge of adrenalin, and she was determined to have a few more goes before leaving to ensure it wasn't just a one-off.

All the other jumps in the field had been put up, and Joanne and Flash tore over them. It was true that Flash jumped better over higher fences, but his style was still rather hair-raising as he bounced sideways, holding himself stiffly erect with his head and neck bolt upright, until the last stride where he snatched the reins and hurtled at the jump. As he took off, he stretched out beautifully and flowed gracefully over the fence like molten copper. Amber watched them enviously.

Concentrating once more on the tiny cross pole, Amber made Pearl go over it another three times before she called it a night. Weary from the effort, she leaned forward and patted Pearl's sweaty neck.

"Thank you Mrs Jones," she puffed breathlessly.

"Oh, call me Lou," said Mrs Jones kindly, waving a hand in the air. "You're very welcome. You did really well for a first try. Well done."

Trudging back up the track to the farm, Mrs Anderson asked Amber if she had enjoyed her first taste of jumping.

Amber looked down into her mother's face. She didn't know what to say, so she merely shrugged her shoulders. The truth was that a silent battle of emotions was taking place within her. She remembered Sapphire, the imaginary pony, on whom she had competed and won. She thought about how thrilled she had felt when she found out that Pearl had been bought for her, and how all her dreams of winning trophies and rosettes had been forgotten in her happiness at having her own pony.

Then she pictured Flash soaring mightily over the fences in the field. Amber looked between Pearl's neat black ears and found herself wishing that she wasn't riding little, fat, stubborn Pearl, but a beautiful, athletic show jumper with spirit and elegance.

An uncomfortable lump formed in her throat as guilt swelled inside her.

"Don't think like that," she chided herself, *"give her a chance. Like Mrs Jones said; a bit of practice and she could easily improve."*

She tried to cheer up and be more hopeful, but there was another little voice in her head that kept creeping in and whispering to her in snide tones, *"Get real. Face the truth. Pearl will never be a jumper, and you know it. Best get used to it."* The voice paused. *"Maybe Pearl isn't the pony for you after all."*

- Eight -

Second Attempt

Amber did not look forward to going riding over the following few days. Usually, she was itching for school to finish so that she could get to Shaw Farm, catch the ponies, give them a brush and set off for a ride.

Now, as the bell went for home time, Amber felt her stomach twist as if a large boulder had just slipped into it and landed with a thud. The heavy weight remained as she climbed into the car next to Mr Anderson.

"Good day at school?" he enquired brightly while handing her a sandwich.

Amber nodded and muttered something incomprehensible before taking a bite of the sandwich and chewing it slowly so that she couldn't join in any conversation her dad might have been thinking of starting. They drove to the farm in silence.

Bumping over the pot-holed farm track past Joanne's house, they noticed Joanne leading Flash out of the paddock. Mr Anderson stopped the car and wound his window down. Leaning out slightly he called up to her. "Are you riding today Joanne?"

She waved and replied, "yeah, stop off for me on your way past."

Flash was his usual self on the ride. He now went slowly enough to allow the riders to have a conversation, but only because he crab-stepped and jogged on the spot, habitually wrenching the reins from his rider.

Joanne ignored him and carried on talking, despite the fact that she kept getting yanked out of the saddle and was constantly having to gather her reins.

"Don't fee- OW, FLASH. Don't feel too disappointed about the other day," she said to Amber, sensing that her friend was rather quiet and solemn-faced, "lots of ponies get confused when they're first introduced to jumping. *You* have to educate her."

Amber gave Joanne a puzzled look.

"I mean practice. I'm sure you can get her moving a bit faster than granny speed!" she laughed. "The more you do it, the better she'll get."

Amber tried to ignore the pessimistic voice inside her saying, *"No she won't,"* and agreed to have another go at jumping.

"It'll have to be Saturday though," gasped Joanne, jabbing Flash in the mouth after a particularly violent snatch, "we've got a competition on Sunday."

They were nearing the bottom of the forestry hill and Flash was prancing and head shaking with deliberate exaggeration. He no longer bolted up the hill from the very bottom, but when he was in a mood like this, he would only wait for so long before he snapped.

"I'd better let him have a gallop," shouted Joanne over her shoulder, "he's so hyped up he's going to go inside out if I don't let him go. See you at the top!" She let her reins slip fractionally and that was all Flash needed. He pounded up the hill like a rocket, sending a shower of pebbles up behind him.

Amber, who was cantering along in Flash's wake next to her dad on Honey, got hit in the face by a pebble flying up from the pony's hind feet. It struck her cheek with such force that she cried out from the sharp, sudden pain. Before she could stop it, that little voice was back again, complaining. *"Oh Pearl, why do you have to be so slow?"*

***

Saturday was pleasantly warm and sunny and Amber felt her spirits lift. Determined to shut out the negative voice in her head, she told herself that Pearl would be much better today now that she knew what to do. And, as Joanne had said, she needed to take small steps and not expect too much.

Mr Anderson was at work, so her mother brought her to the farm and was helping to tack Pearl up. She looked at her daughter, small worry lines creasing her brow.

"Now dear," she began quietly, "you won't get…er… *upset* if Pearl doesn't go well today will you?" She stopped adjusting the bridle and looked over Pearl's neck to see Amber, who was pulling up the girth. "Remember, horses are like people, and they have their likes and dislikes. You don't like maths, and maybe Pearl doesn't like jumping…" her voice trailed away.

"I'm glad you're being *so* encouraging," replied Amber sarcastically without looking up from the girth.

"Hey now, no need for that attitude. I'm not trying to put you off," Mrs Anderson said quickly, "I'm just trying to prepare you for…well, you know. Pearl has been a trekking pony all her life. She's not used to all this…we never bought her as a jumping pony," she trailed off, mumbling the final words to herself.

***

The jumps were set as cross poles or low straight poles. Matthew was warming up on Sam when Amber and Mrs Anderson arrived.

They noticed that Joanne was missing. Flash's eager chestnut head looked out of his stable door, his white blaze gleaming in the sunlight. His nostrils quivered, and he stood stock still, like a frozen statue before emitting an ear-splitting scream. A low answering whinny came from the jumping field which seemed to act as a key to unlock Flash from his stupor. The erratic pony began frantically weaving and banging the door with his chest and legs. Joanne came scurrying from the tack room and shut the top door of the stable so that Flash could no longer see out into the yard.

"Just keep *quiet* in there," she shouted through the door at him. "Oh hi," she said, noticing that Amber had arrived, "Matthew's practising. He's doing ten and under solo jumping tomorrow. I'm not doing anything with him today," she inclined her head towards the now quiet stable that held Flash, "he'll have his fun tomorrow."

Amber entered the jumping paddock where Matthew, watched by Mrs Jones, had begun to go over the small fences. She saw Amber and waved but did not come across to speak as she was shouting advice to Matthew. "Remember to use your legs! Don't look *at* the jump, look *beyond* it," she said while thrusting her finger in the air to indicate where Matthew should be looking.

Amber shortened her stirrups as she had been shown and let Pearl trot and canter a few circuits of the field before she began. She knew Joanne and her own mother were watching her, but this time it didn't make her feel nervous. Instead Amber was determined to prove that she and Pearl could jump.

She turned her pony towards the cross pole that had caused her so much trouble on their last attempt. Pearl broke from canter back into a trot but Amber dug her heels into Pearl's sides and gave her a smart tap on the shoulder with her riding crop. Surprised, Pearl quickened her pace and jumped the fence from a fast trot.

"Try some others," Joanne called from where she was watching with Mrs Anderson, who was looking rather relieved.

Amber headed again for the same cross pole and jumped it easily from a steady trot. On landing, she steered Pearl round to the left, towards a low straight pole balanced on top of two lemonade crates. Again, Pearl tried to back off, but another quick dig from Amber's heels sent her up to and over the jump. She continued around the field and jumped every fence in both directions.

Pearl had never got faster than a trot, but it had been hard work keeping her going. Amber gave Pearl a hearty pat. She knew the jumps were only tiny, but still, it was progress, and she was pleased. Feelings of warmth and love towards her pony flooded back into her again, washing away every negative and nasty thought she'd recently had. She could see everyone was smiling at her as she rode towards the edge of the field.

"That was great Amber," said Mrs Jones warmly, "you rode really positively. Well done."

Amber glowed with pride at such praise.

Joanne ran ahead to open the gate, her short blonde pony-tail bouncing as she moved.

As Amber rode through the gate, an idea popped into Joanne's head. "I know," she exclaimed. "Why don't you come and watch me at the show tomorrow? You'll see what goes on and how everything works in case you ever want to have a go yourself. Will you come?"

Amber looked at her mother, who shrugged her shoulders. She knew that meant it was up to her to choose. Amber thought for a second then said, "yeah we'll come. It's the field on Watch Hill isn't it?"

Joanne nodded and grinned, "See you there then!"

– Nine –

A Decision is Made

The show field was already packed with brightly coloured horseboxes and an assortment of trailers by the time Amber and her parents arrived. Children on ponies of all shapes and sizes were milling around, from absolute tots on their little Shetlands who were being led around by harassed looking mums or dads, to children of about her own age – mostly girls – on ponies that looked lean, fit and purposeful.

Amber scanned the grounds trying to catch a glimpse of the Jones'. They walked further into the hubbub, carefully keeping out of the way of children who were cantering their ponies in all directions, apparently not looking where they were going. Eventually, Amber spotted the Jones' bright green lorry and signalled to her parents to follow her.

Flash was tied up to the side of the lorry. The restless pony swung his body relentlessly from one side to another, trying to get a better look at Sam, who stood a little way off.

Matthew was mounted, and Mrs Jones was giving his boots a last-minute polish. Beside her stood a man that Amber had never seen before. She assumed he was Joanne's father due to him having curly brown hair like Matthew's.

Her parents shook hands with him as Mrs Jones introduced everyone.

"Jo's around somewhere dear," Mrs Jones stated, still fervently rubbing Matthew's boots, "she went to put her entries in and she's probably found someone to talk to. She'll be back soon to watch Matthew. His class starts in five minutes."

As if suddenly realising that five minutes was not a very long time, Mrs Jones stopped rubbing and started fussing about finding the practice jump and getting ready.

The show jumping arena contained ten professional looking jumps with white wings and brightly coloured poles – like the ones at Hickstead, only considerably smaller. At the moment the jumps were about 65cm and ready for Matthew's class, which was for children who were ten years or under and could ride the course without assistance.

Amber and her parents positioned themselves where they had a good view of all the jumps. She caught a glimpse of Matthew and Sam neatly jumping the practice fence amongst the other competitors in his class who were also collecting in the warm-up area. Mr and Mrs Jones were standing near the entrance and Amber could see that Joanne was with them, standing next to a girl with long dark hair.

The first competitor entered the arena. The commentator announced her and the pony's name and blew a whistle. The girl, who only looked about seven years old was riding a pretty skewbald pony. She pushed her riding hat up out of her eyes and began. She did very well, just having one pole off the second part of the double.

"That's four faults for Katie," the commentator boomed. Several more competitors had their turn and Amber watched intently, paying close attention to the commentator's scoring of each round. So far, she had learnt that a competitor got four faults for a knockdown, or if the pony refused a jump. If the pony refused twice, the competitor was eliminated, which meant they had to leave the ring without completing their round.

"Next into the arena can we have Matthew Jones riding Samurai."

Amber watched with greater interest as Matthew rode into the arena. On the other side, the Jones' watched anxiously. Matthew looked twice the size he usually did encased in his body protector, but he still sat quietly and in balance with his pony as he cantered around the jumps, waiting for the whistle to signal the start of his round.

The whistle sounded, and Matthew brought Sam round to the first jump, which was comprised of green and yellow poles. Sam hopped over happily with a swish of his tail and continued around the remaining nine jumps in the same easy, steady rhythm ensuring a nice clear round for Matthew.

At the end of the class there were five clear rounds. The commentator announced that there would now be a jump-off over a shortened course to decide the placings.

There was a pause while some other adults came into the arena and put some of the jumps up a hole. The commentator then told the competitors the jump-off course and asked the first rider, Jennifer Scott riding Oakbank Delta Dream, to come into the arena.

Amber watched as the competitors tackled the jump-off in a completely different way to the first round. In the jump-off they had to go as fast as possible, as the clear round with the fastest time won. She was amazed to see how some of the ponies were able to land after a jump and, without even taking a stride, could turn immediately to cut inside and take a shortened route to the next jump. She was in awe of the riding abilities of these young children and wondered if she would ever get to their level.

Matthew was the last competitor to go in the class. Three out of the previous four riders had gone clear so the class was going to be won on time. Would Matthew go for it she wondered? As it turned out, he did not push Sam for speed, but because his pony was so steady and balanced, he was one of the few that could turn immediately on landing and take much shorter routes around the course.

When his time was called out at the end of his round, he had come second. Everyone clapped as the five riders lined up to be presented with their rosettes and cantered away in a lap of honour around the arena. The Jones' whooped and clapped for their son as he made his way around.

The next jumping class was for ponies under 12.2hh and neither Matthew nor Joanne were in that class. The Andersons went to congratulate Matthew and find out when Joanne would be riding.

At the lorry, Sam was untacked and tucking into his hay net while Joanne was in the process of putting something into Flash's shoes. The dark-haired girl who had been with Joanne earlier was sitting on the steps into the lorry.

"Haven't you seen studs before?" she said, looking directly at Amber, who had her head on one side, trying to see what Joanne was doing.

"No, what are they for?" asked Amber.

The girl rolled her eyes and tossed her dark hair. Getting up off the step she paused to say, "See you later," to Joanne before stalking off.

Surprised by the girl's rudeness, Amber asked Joanne who she was.

"That's Elisha Templeton," replied Joanne, still fiddling with Flash's feet, "she does British Showjumping. She's got fabulous ponies."

"Oh right," replied Amber, feeling stupid for not knowing what studs or British Showjumping were, but not wanting to ask. "Are you riding soon?"

"I'm in the next class. Are you going to watch?" Joanne asked.

"Yeah, good luck,"

"Thanks."

Joanne's class was for ponies of 13.2hh or under. Flash was eligible as he was 13hh. The jumps were now higher than they had been for Matthew's class and brightly coloured fillers had been placed under some of the jumps.

As the competitors took their turn in the ring, Amber noticed that all the ponies seemed to enjoy what they were doing. They were all forward going and some of them leapt and pulled just like Flash. The riders coped expertly with their exuberant mounts.

"And the next competitor is Joanne Jones on Flash Dance."

As soon as Flash heard the whistle, he put his head down and seized the bit. Joanne managed to get him pointing at the first fence before he bolted towards it, clearing it with an unnecessarily high jump. He continued around the full course in this manner with Joanne just about managing to steer him, although there were a couple of moments where it looked like he was going to come out over the arena rope. Somehow, she managed to keep him on the correct course and they got a clear round. Fortunately, there were several clears, so she could have a rest before she had to deal with the jump-off.

Amber watched the jump-off, which was won by a pony that jumped slowly like Sam. It made the most incredible twists and turns and finished with a much faster time than the other ponies. Joanne had come fourth as Flash was just so difficult to control that she had to go wide around all the fences and lost a lot of time, even though Flash was flying.

She congratulated Joanne as she left the ring with her green rosette, but her friend seemed sullen and disappointed, and rode past without speaking, her eyes hard and her jaw set.

Amber couldn't believe that she'd been snubbed so rudely and just stared at the retreating back of Joanne as she rode moodily back to the lorry.

She felt a hand on her shoulder which gently steered her away. "Come on love, best to leave her to sulk in private." Tearing her eyes away from Joanne who had now dismounted and flung her riding hat angrily on the floor, she went with her parents to look at the other events taking place.

They saw the handy pony competition, where the riders had to manoeuvre their ponies through various scary obstacles like flapping bags and spinning windmills and were timed on how fast they completed the obstacles. They also saw some of the Pony Club games, which looked like great fun. The riders galloped through bending poles, and the ponies were clearly aware that they were racing each other.

When the time came to leave and they were walking back to the car, Amber thought back to the jumping classes she had watched that had both been won by slower, more sensible ponies. She felt hope brewing inside.

"Can I join the Pony Club?" she asked.

Her parents exchanged worried looks. "Are you sure dear? I mean, you can if you want to, certainly, but…well, Pearl is not like the ponies you've seen here today. She might do ok, but she'll never be a winner."

Amber was undeterred. "I'm sure," she said decisively. "Let's join today."

– Jen –

Pony Club Rally

The District Commissioner of the Blakefield branch of the Pony Club was a large, jolly woman with a ruddy, weather worn complexion. She was delighted to have a new member and told Amber and her parents that their next gymkhana would take place in two weeks. In the meantime, there was a rally on Thursday evening.

"We do insist that all members take part in at least two ridden rallies a year," she informed them eloquently. "We also have stable management rallies in winter. The dress code for rallies is light coloured jodhpurs, a shirt, Pony Club tie and the Pony Club sweatshirt. Obviously, we will order these for you but you won't have them by Thursday.

You can come in normal riding wear, so long as it is safe, for your first rally."

"But Mrs…" Amber started but blushed and stopped as she'd forgotten her name.

"Mrs Best, dear, Mrs Best," she reminded her heartily.

"We don't have a horsebox or anything to get here," explained Amber, worrying that her failure to attend the rally would incur the wrath of this bombastic woman.

"We'll ask Lou. Their horsebox is stalled to carry three so they'll have room if they're coming," suggested Mr Anderson quickly.

"Splendid," boomed Mrs Best. "Well, I'll look forward to seeing you there then."

***

Joanne and Matthew were going to the rally and it was arranged that Pearl would be taken to the Pony Club field in their lorry while the Andersons followed in their car.

When Amber led Pearl into the Jones' yard to load her into their lorry, she noticed that Flash and Sam both wore long, padded boots on their legs. A bandage covered their tails and both ponies wore a light rug, despite the warmth of the day. Pearl was completely bare, wearing only her headcollar. Amber felt a tug of worry. She hadn't known that ponies wore such things to protect them from bumps and rubs while they were travelling.

"Not to worry," Mrs Jones reassured her when she mentioned it. "She'll be alright for this journey. We'll take it nice and steady, but you might want to think about getting her some travelling gear for future trips."

With Flash and Sam both loaded in the box, came Pearl's turn. Amber felt nervous as she stepped up the ramp in case Pearl refused to go in. Unused to being asked to walk up a steep ramp into a dark, unknown space, the pony hesitated and gave a deep uncertain snort. Amber didn't rush her. She let her sniff the ramp and patted her neck to soothe her. Reassured, Pearl soon followed Amber like a lamb and took her place in the end stall beside Sam.

***

The rally took place at the same field as the gymkhana. As they tacked up, Amber noticed how smart everyone looked in their cream jodhpurs and the red

Blakefield Pony Club sweater. She felt quite out of place in her black jodhpurs and plain green sweatshirt.

Joanne and Matthew seemed to know exactly what to do and trotted off to join the riders that were circling in different corners of the field.

There were four groups moving around; from the smallest lead rein children to the fourth group which was made up of older teenagers, who were mostly riding impressively large and powerful horses. Matthew had joined the second group that contained young riders who could ride independently, while Joanne had gone to the third group, where the riders were older and the ponies generally bigger than those in Matthew's group.

Amber noticed that Joanne was riding around next to Elisha, the girl with the 'fabulous ponies' who had been with her on Sunday. Elisha's pony was an athletic, long-legged and slender-necked mahogany bay. It was bigger than Flash and walked with a regal air, arching its neck and stepping delicately with dainty feet.

Amber mounted and rode over to join Joanne and Elisha. Everyone in that group seemed to be from about ten to thirteen years old so she assumed she would also be with them. However, when the instructor saw that Amber had joined the ride, she quietly went over to her and explained that the groups were organised by ability and experience as well as age. As Amber was not very experienced, the instructor kindly told her that she would be in the second group.

Amber turned Pearl away with her eyes to the ground and her cheeks flushing pink. As she left, Amber heard Elisha laugh and say, "As if she could be in this group on *that*."

Hurt and humiliated, Amber joined the second group, where she was by far the oldest rider. She didn't have time to feel sorry for herself for very long though as the young, enthusiastic instructor had them line up ready to go.

Amber soon found herself swinging her body around the saddle and sitting backwards so that she was looking down at Pearl's tail instead of through her ears. She practised mounting and dismounting from both sides and lying back along Pearl's spine while seated in the saddle. Next, some small jumps were put out in a line called a 'bounce'. That meant that as soon as the pony landed over one fence, it would have to jump again without taking a stride. The children rode down the line of jumps one after another with Pearl at the end so that she could follow the others.

Amber found herself laughing with joy as Pearl hopped over the jumps, one after another. At the end of the rally, she'd had so much fun that she completely forgot about Elisha's spitefulness. She couldn't wait to get to her first show.

– Eleven –

Amber's First Show

Show day arrived quickly, and Amber fizzed with excitement as they loaded the car with all the new things they had bought: a show jacket, body protector, leather jodhpur boots, gloves and a numnah and girth for Pearl.

Amber swelled with pride when she saw how smart her pony looked. She had long protective boots over her legs and a thick tail guard bulged against the bushy tail it encased.

Mr Anderson had managed to borrow a small pony sized trailer from a friend at work who only used it occasionally to move a few sheep from one field to another, so they were going by themselves to the gymkhana.

"It's no good putting on people's hospitality," Mr Anderson had said. "If we're going to do this, we'll do it ourselves instead of relying on other people."

As they drove off down the track, the trailer bumping along behind them, and Honey squealing from the field after her departed companion, Amber began to feel a strange sensation in her stomach. She definitely wanted to go but she couldn't help but worry about what was to come in the day ahead.

"I do hope Pearl behaves," she thought, silently staring out of the window.

***

The show field looked just as it had last time, with rows of stationary horseboxes and trailers. Mr Anderson found a space and parked. They unloaded Pearl and tied her to the side of the trailer while her boots were removed. Pearl had a look round as if trying to work out where she was, then with a sigh, put her head down to graze.

Leaving Mr Anderson to keep an eye on her, Amber and her mother went to find out where to place the entries.

They soon found a small caravan with a queue of people waiting outside the door and looking at a board next to the caravan. Getting nearer, they could see that the board held the schedule for the day.

Scanning the classes that were available Mrs Anderson said, "Well you might as well have a go at everything while you're here. The jumping doesn't start for a bit, and they're only doing the lead rein equitation at the moment, so you can do that while you're waiting for the jumping to start. It'll get Pearl warmed up."

Amber, who had been reading the schedule closely, said in a slightly panicked voice, "I don't think I'll be doing the jumping. The class Pearl should be in is 85cm. There's no way she'll jump that. They're the fences Joanne was doing on Flash last time."

"Oh…well, that's a shame. We'll ask about that."

They got in the queue to place their entries and when it was their turn, Mrs Anderson placed Amber's entries for equitation, handy pony and games.

"Rider's name?" asked the lady who was taking the entries.

"Amber Anderson," her mum replied.

"And what's the pony's name?"

"Pearl," Mrs Anderson replied.

"No, *wait*," Amber interrupted frantically. "People don't call the pony by its home name at shows, they have a special name for when they are competing," she cried, remembering some of the names from last week. "We need a show name for Pearl."

"How about Little Pearl?" suggested Mrs Anderson, "that's what they used to call her at the riding school remember? Claire had that old retired horse called Pearl as well. They used to call them Big Pearl and Little Pearl so that they knew which one was which. Little Pearl sounds nice don't you think?"

"Yeah, that's what she'll be called." Amber told the lady. "Put her down as Little Pearl."

Before they paid the entry fee, Mrs Anderson explained that Amber was worried about the height of the jumps in her class and asked if there was anything else she could do.

"She could go in the class before that; the 12.2hh class. The jumps will be a maximum height of 75cm but she will have to go hors concours, or non-competitively, which just means that she won't get a rosette if she gets placed," explained the entry lady.

They agreed that this was a better idea, even though 75cm was still bigger than Pearl had jumped before.

Amber's first event was equitation. There were nine riders in the class, most of whom had obviously spent a long time preparing. The ponies' coats gleamed, their manes and tails were neatly plaited and the riders themselves were immaculate. Amber had cleaned all Pearl's tack the night before, given her a thorough groom and polished her own boots until she could see her reflection in them. But Amber worried that she would be told off by the judge, who was already sweeping her critical eye over the riders as they walked around her in a circle, for not having her pony plaited.

The riders were soon asked to move up into a trot and then canter as the judge continued to scrutinise them. Presently, they were asked to line up alongside each other. The judge walked in front, examining each of them for cleanliness. This judge was very particular. She looked at the underside of the stirrups, the inside of the bridle straps and reins, under the saddle flaps and she even lifted the ponies' feet to check they were clean. Amber was glad she had picked out and oiled Pearl's hooves.

As the judge finally approached her, Amber felt that she had to apologise for not being plaited up.

"Doesn't really apply in your case though," the judge muttered absently as she ran her fingers through Pearl's mane searching for tangles. Finding none, she moved to Pearl's head to inspect her bridle, "since your pony is a native breed. Natives should always be shown in their natural state." She gave Pearl one last look over then walked away, scribbling something on her clipboard.

Next, each rider had to perform an individual show. The judge asked them to show walk, trot and canter on both reins, and if they could manage it, a rein back or turn on the forehand. Amber was glad she was last in line as she was able to watch and see what everyone else did. She noticed how they all saluted the judge at the end of their show and made a mental note to remember to do so.

The fifth pony to come out of the line to do its show was the beautiful mahogany bay ridden by the acidic Elisha. Amber hadn't noticed that she was in the class. Her pony behaved impeccably. Just like at the rally, it stepped daintily, skimming over the ground with slender legs and an arched neck. The rein back at the end was perfect; the pony was completely obedient and didn't object once. She saluted smartly and smiled winningly at the judge before moving back into line. Elisha then looked down to where she and Pearl stood, and Amber was sure she smirked at her before disappearing back into the line of ponies.

Finally, as the penultimate pony completed its show and returned to its place beside Pearl, it was Amber's turn. Remembering everything she had watched, she nudged Pearl to move forward. Pearl, who had been standing idle for several minutes and had started to doze, moved forward sluggishly. Amber had to give her a hearty thump with the leg the judge couldn't see to wake her up. Pearl walked and trotted amiably on both reins, but she really could not be bothered to canter. Amber worked furiously to get her going, but each time she managed only a couple of strides before falling back into a trot. Out of the corner of her eye, she could make out the blurred figure of Elisha sitting pretty on her perfect pony. She could imagine the look on her face as she watched Amber's show.

Red-faced and flustered, Amber decided to give up on the canter and get out of everyone's sight. She quickly performed her rein back, which Pearl managed with only a trace of resistance, saluted and hurried back into the line feeling hot and bothered.

Amber followed on as the other riders went back into a circle and rode around while the judge looked at her clipboard then glanced up to look at the riders again. She started calling numbers out. Amber noticed that Elisha was first to be called out. She took her place at the head of the line with a smug look on her face. Other numbers were called out for second place, third, fourth, and fifth until there was only one place left with four riders still remaining.

"Eighty-Seven," called the judge.

It took Amber a moment to realise that was her number – she had been given a square of white cardboard with the number in black when she placed her entries, and was now wearing it on her back, tied around her waist with a piece of black string.

As she took her place at the end of the line, a huge grin spread over her face. She couldn't believe she had been placed. She looked at the three riders left behind. They all looked upset. Amber felt for them but at the same time was glad she wasn't amongst them. She was going to get her first rosette!

The judge moved down the line, presenting rosettes and commenting on the riders' performances. When she got to Amber, she handed her a lovely purple rosette and said, "Congratulations, you ride very well, and you have nice light hands. You could do with using more seat and leg as your pony lacks impulsion."

"Right, thanks," replied Amber, not quite sure what she meant, but sure it was about Pearl's reluctance to canter.

Everyone was delighted with Pearl's first rosette, but Amber was still worried about the challenge ahead.

Joanne congratulated Amber and offered to walk the course with her. As they walked around the fences, Amber found that she was too nervous to concentrate on the advice.

"You need to come deep into the corner for this one to get a good stride," Joanne explained while pointing to the fence. "This is a two-stride double, but if Pearl is only trotting, you'll need to kick on, so she can get out over the second part."

Amber wasn't really listening to Joanne's words of advice. She just wanted to concentrate on the order of the jumps so she didn't go the wrong way. The first two or three weren't so intimidating, but some of the others worried her a bit as they were far bigger than what they had practised in Joanne's field.

They left the arena and Amber found her father, who was holding Pearl in the collecting ring. She got on apprehensivley and began to warm-up. The practice jump was a low cross pole and other competitors were already going over it on their ponies. Amber moved in behind the others and followed them. She rode Pearl up to the jump and to her relief, she popped over it without hesitation.

"That's it, Pearl, we can do this," she laughed, giving her pony an appreciative pat on the neck.

As Amber turned and approached for another go at the practice fence, she saw that it had quickly been put up to a much higher straight pole. She kicked on and hoped for the best as they approached the jump. Pearl's ears pricked forward as if she too had noticed the new proportions of the fence in front of her. Deciding that it was far too big, Pearl dug her heels in and stopped. Time seemed to slow as she skidded slightly and knocked the pole with her chest so that it fell down on the ground in front of them.

"Oh *great*," a voice came from behind. A small boy on a bouncy bay pony had been about to follow Amber over the jump. He nearly crashed into the back of her as he struggled to pull his pony out of the way.

"Dad, come and put this jump up!" the boy demanded.

By the time the fence had been erected and people were happily flying over it once again, the commentator had announced the start of the class. Amber was mortified to discover that she was the first to go.

"And this is our first competitor," said the commentator, in his sonorous amplified voice. "Amber Anderson riding Little Pearl. This competitor is riding hors concours."

The whistle blew. Amber gathered up her reins and gave Pearl a tap on the shoulder to show her that she meant business. Pearl cantered down the long side of the arena but upon seeing the first jump, fell back to a trot. Amber kicked hard and shouted at Pearl as they approached the jump. "Go *on*," she pleaded. Pearl slowed down and was practically ambling, but just as Amber thought that was it, Pearl managed to jump the fence from a near standstill. She jumped the next two fences in a similar fashion with Amber encouraging her in every way possible. The fourth jump was a bit bigger than the previous three and had a little spread on it. She tried hard but Pearl just seemed to run out of steam in front of it.

Amber turned, fully aware that another stop would mean elimination.

"Get over it," she commanded through gritted teeth as they came round for the second attempt.

Amber kicked madly all the way up to the fence, and sensing that her rider was feeling particularly determined, Pearl gathered herself and jumped.

Had she been going faster, everything would have been fine, but as she had taken the jump as slowly as usual, she caught the back pole of the spread with her hind feet. As she landed, the pole came down between her back legs and caused her to stumble. Amber lost her balance and was thrown forward onto Pearl's neck. She sat up quickly and tried to gather her reins back up but with the next fence so close and with her rider's reins too long, and her position out of balance, Pearl seized the opportunity to duck past the jump. The whistle blew immediately.

"I'm sorry, but that's elimination. You may jump a fence on your way out."

Feeling absolutely dismal, Amber turned Pearl towards the first fence again, which she, of course, jumped sweetly.

As she left the collecting ring, she noticed Joanne standing with Elisha. They had seen everything.

"Fancy getting eliminated over jumps as small as those. How pathetic is *that*?" Elisha laughed.

Without waiting to hear Joanne's reply, she fled back to the trailer in tears.

"That's it. I'm *done*. I've had enough of this lazy pony and these stuck-up girls," Amber sobbed.

But her mother was stern. "You can't just throw in the towel because your first attempt wasn't successful. You *know* Pearl has never jumped; you're expecting too much of her, and yourself." Mrs Anderson turned to Pearl and placed a comforting hand between her eyes. "If you really want to do it, you need to start having jumping lessons because you've both got a lot to learn. Neither of you can rely on the other because neither of you knows what you're doing. You can look forward to learning together. Now, you're entered for games and handy pony and I've paid, so you're going to cheer up and take part."

Amber was quite surprised that her parents weren't more sympathetic, but she knew, deep down that her mother's words of wisdom were true. It was wrong to blame Pearl. She *did* need to have lessons again if she was serious about it. Feeling slightly less despondent, they all made their way down to the next event.

***

Handy pony turned out to be Pearl's forte. While the flapping tape, large cuddly toys, plastic bags to walk over and various other frightening obstacles caused endless problems to many competitors' ponies, they were nothing to Pearl, the suddenly fearless pony. The endless hours they'd spent at home teaching the ponies to think for themselves and be more independent had clearly paid off as she didn't bat an eyelid at anything on the course and Amber finished everything easily.

"That was an excellent time," said the organiser, looking at his stopwatch. "I can't tell you what position you're in, but let's just say you're doing well." He winked and smiled. "That's a very brave pony you've got there. One of the best I've seen all day. Well done."

Amber smiled. This was one event where Pearl could shine.

Games could not begin for Amber's age group yet because the other riders entered for it were still jumping. While they were waiting, the Andersons left Pearl grazing by the trailer, took their sandwiches and went to watch the jumping.

The 13.2hh class had finished when they got there but they could see Joanne in the collecting ring. Flash was sporting a yellow rosette showing that she had come third. The jumps now looked very imposing as the 14.2hh class was about to start.

They watched in awe as the ponies thundered around the arena, soaring gracefully over the jumps. There were a few poles down and the odd refusal, but no-one was eliminated.

Amber watched with resentment as Elisha steered two ponies to clear rounds. One was the dark bay she had already seen. He was called 'North Quest' and jumped as neatly and politely as he went on the flat. The other was a burning chestnut, much darker and brighter than Flash; like smouldering flames in a fire; and was called 'Red Revenge'. He was not as pretty as North Quest, having a sturdy, powerful body and a bigger, more robust head, but he was bold and precise and produced an energetic clear round.

The jump-off, which was very exciting, was won by Elisha on Red Revenge. He was fast and strong, but also able to make quick turns and jump from tricky angles that meant he was well in the lead. North Quest was slower but perfectly obedient, so he lost no ground and was also able to cut in and save time. He came in third. Amber didn't know any of the other riders who were placed.

The last class was Open Pony, where any size of pony could enter. But as the jumps were now over a metre, there were only five entries. Elisha was riding her two ponies, and Joanne was going in on Flash. Alongside them were two other girls; one on a 14.2hh that had been placed in the previous round and the other on a 13.2hh. As the class wasn't going to take very long, the Andersons went back to the trailer to get Pearl ready for games.

Open Pony finished with Elisha in the first two positions and Joanne third. Now that all the pony jumping had finished, the riders began to assemble for games. Joanne was there and to Amber's dismay, Elisha also turned up on the chestnut pony. There were three other riders, all of whom were riding spirited looking ponies.

The riders lined up for the first race: bending. The starter's flag went up and all eyes watched intently as riders sat poised in the saddle and ponies fidgeted with excitement. The flag fell, and five ponies spurted from the start line straight into a flat-out gallop through the line of bending poles.

Pearl did not move as the flag fell.

Amber kicked and shouted desperately, but Pearl could only be roused into her usual steady trot. By the time she reached the top bending pole, all the other ponies had finished.

The next two races, flag and mug, went just as the first had. The other ponies seemed to be watching the starter's flag and leapt off the start line as soon as it fell. Pearl, on the other hand, did everything at her own pace. She was deadly accurate and Amber never missed a flag or a mug, but she finished considerably later than everyone else. As they waited to get their rosettes, Elisha pursed her lips and gave Amber a pitying look.

"Aww, you haven't had a very good day, have you?" she mocked.

"It's only her first time," said Joanne, seeing the colour rising in Amber's face.

"It wouldn't matter if it were her hundredth time on *that* thing," she said, turning her nose up at Pearl. "She'll never do anything on that...whatever it is. I don't think it's even purebred."

A silent scream rose in Amber's throat. She tried desperately to think of something witty and cutting to say to this horrid person in front of her, but she could think of nothing. She felt the threat of tears rising in her eyes, and not wanting Elisha to see that she'd made her cry, turned and went back to the trailer without waiting for her rosette.

"Leave her alone Elisha," Joanne told her friend quietly, looking after Amber's slumped form as she rode away.

Elisha smiled to herself and said nothing.

– Twelve –

Elisha's Challenge

Amber burned with disappointment. It didn't matter that she won the handy pony; Pearl still felt like a failure. As a result, the Andersons decided that she wouldn't compete again for the rest of the season until Member's Cup. Instead, she was to attend rallies and start having regular lessons again, focusing particularly on jumping.

***

It felt strange to be back at Pine Tree now that Pearl belonged to her.

Claire was a good teacher; patient but unrelenting. Amber had expected to be jumping straight away but Claire said there was a lot to do before they could even think about jumps. Amber felt completely dispirited when, for weeks, she had to practise walking around the arena in a two-point seat. Then she had to do it in trot. At first, she couldn't hold herself in position for more than a few seconds without flopping back into the saddle but as her strength and balance improved, so did her position. Next, they worked on Pearl's canter transition and on keeping her going. Claire made Amber repeat each aspect of the lesson over and over until it was perfect. At the end of an hour, her muscles ached all over from the effort of coaxing Pearl to work hard.

Although the lessons were demanding for both girl and pony, they were beginning to pay off. Amber now had a much more secure seat and lower leg position. Pearl still had her own unique way of slowing right down in front of a fence before jumping it, but they were now managing full courses of 75cm, including doubles. Amber was delighted with Pearl and itching to get to Member's Cup and show Elisha what they could do. Mrs Best had told them the jumps for her age group at Member's Cup would be 75 to 80cm and Amber felt confident that they could now get round the course.

Member's Cup was still three weeks away, however, and was the last event of the season. For the coming weekend, a fun ride had been organised for the members in the countryside near where Mrs Best lived, and Amber was looking forward to the day.

***

Sunday arrived, dull and moody after a stormy Saturday night. The clouds were low and dark, but it was dry. Amber made sure she dressed warmly in her waterproof jacket. It looked like they might be in for some heavy downpours.

When they arrived at the venue, Amber was given a reflective tabard and a sheet of paper with the directions for the ride.

"You needn't worry too much about these," the lady flustered, trying to stop directions flying away in the wind, "everybody will go around in twos or threes, and the route is marked clearly with tape, so you can't get lost."

Amber put on her tabard, mounted and went to find Joanne. To her dismay, she found her friend sitting on Flash right next to Elisha on her chestnut pony.

"Oh no, not her again," Amber groaned inwardly. Feeling like a bucket of ice had just entered her stomach, she rode over to join them.

"Oh no, I don't *think* so," Elisha spat as Amber joined them. "You are *not* coming with us."

Amber looked at Joanne.

"I said I'd ride with her," replied Joanne meekly. "I didn't know you were coming."

"Well I'm here, and I'm *not* riding with her. She'll totally spoil the day on that tortoise." She looked down her nose at Pearl and grimaced.

Joanne looked towards Amber and shrugged her shoulders. "Sorry," she said simply, her eyes to the ground.

Amber was speechless. She couldn't believe Joanne would treat her like this; that she would bow so subserviently to malicious Elisha.

"Thanks, *friend*," Amber said coldly, emphasising the last word to let Joanne know exactly how she felt. Joanne blushed and kept her eyes down.

Amber turned Pearl, rode away and stood on her own, fighting back the tears that threatened to come once more.

Just as she was regaining her composure but wondering what she was going to do, Mrs Best bounded over.

"Now then, now then," she proclaimed cheerfully, "what's this? A rider sitting on her own, and our new girl too. Is nobody looking after you?"

"I…I thought I was riding with Joanne, but Elisha won't let me go with them." Amber sniffed, valiantly keeping the tears back.

"Oh, I say. She won't will she, little madam. I'd like to know when she became the leader of this Pony Club." Mrs Best's ruddy face turned deep crimson as she thundered over towards Elisha.

Amber wasn't exactly sure what Mrs Best said to Elisha as she kept out of the way, but there was a lot of shouting and finger wagging going on.

Mrs Best came storming back to Amber, trembling and agitated and told her to go and join the two girls. Joanne looked sheepish and rather ashamed, while Elisha shot her a murderous glance and muttered something again about the ride being spoiled. Amber pretended not to hear – but it hurt.

The riders set out in twos and threes down a grassy track and through an open gate. Mrs Best's husband acted as the starter and was setting the riders off at five-minute intervals so that everyone didn't end up in a dangerously large clump. Amber's group ended up being the last one to start out, giving Elisha another reason to scowl.

They set off in total silence, downhill towards the woods. The track came to an end at an open field but the way was blocked by a gate. There was nobody there to open it for them.

"You can do the gate," snapped Elisha. "These two won't stand still so you might as well make yourself useful."

Without speaking, Amber steered her pony over to the gate. Pearl stood quietly while she released the catch and pushed it open. After everyone walked through, Amber closed the gate quickly and efficiently. The fact that she had managed the gate so well only seemed to antagonise Elisha more.

"Let's have a race over this field," she challenged, "to see who's fastest between Flash and Rocky. I bet Flash can't beat Rocky. I bet he doesn't even come close." She seemed to have fallen out with Joanne now and was provoking her so-called friend by insulting her pony. Amber knew exactly how that felt.

Joanne, perfectly confident in Flash's speed, accepted the challenge. Without waiting for further discussion, Elisha jabbed her pony sharply with her heels and he plunged into a gallop. Flash didn't need to be told – as soon as he saw the other chestnut pony racing away from him, he followed in hot pursuit. Amber went after them in a canter, but the field was long and also inclined steeply uphill. She knew Pearl would be tired by the time they got halfway, sooner if she pushed her too fast. She looked up to see the two battling ponies were over half way up. Amber was pleased to see that Flash was winning.

Suddenly a tremendous roar erupted from the sky as an RAF jet on a low flying exercise came streaking out from the ominously dark clouds. It thundered over them and disappeared just as quickly as it had come, an ear-splitting roar resonating in its wake. The unexpected arrival of the jet did not concern Pearl. She flicked her ears back in annoyance at the nerve-jangling sound, but that was her only reaction.

But unlike the rock steady Pearl, the two ponies still galloping up the hill were both completely terrified by the jet and bolted in panic, increasing their pace to a blistering speed. Amber watched incredulously as Flash and Rocky, racing each other and racing from their own terror, vanished from sight over the brow of the hill at breakneck speed. At that moment, the clouds burst, and a torrential downpour began.

"Well this is just great," thought Amber urging Pearl to trot faster, worried that she might become separated from her companions.

As she reached the top of the hill and found that it fell away just as steeply on the other side, Amber had to screw her eyes up against the sheet of rain to try and see into the distance. She blinked and shook her head as the image in front of her cleared. Something was lying at the bottom of the hill.

It was Flash.

There was no sign of Joanne, Elisha or Rocky.

– Thirteen –

999

For a moment Amber couldn't move. She just sat there at the top of the hill, peering through the rain in disbelief at Flash's prone form.

Then it hit her – she had to do something. She spurred Pearl on and they slithered downwards.

The hill was slippery and thick with mud, but Pearl never faltered. How many times had she scolded her pony for being lazy? At that moment, she was incredibly grateful for her slow and steady companion.

Feeling sick with shock she jumped off Pearl and ran to where Flash lay. As she got nearer, she could see there was a barbed wire fence at the bottom of the hill. The riders' route was clearly marked as turning right and following the fence along the field, but as Flash had been going so fast down the hill, he had been unable to stop or turn. He'd had no choice but to try and jump over the razor-sharp wire. Amber could see from the deep skid marks that he had tried to slow down to set himself up to jump but had slid on the rain-slicked ground as he took off. Consequently, he hadn't been able to make the height and had gone through the fence rather than over it. Now he lay tangled in wire where he had fallen.

Scrambling over the broken fence, she was repulsed to find an arm sticking out from under the pony's body. Amber gasped as she realised that Joanne was trapped. Panic rushed through her body. *"What should I do? And where on earth are Elisha and Rocky?"* Physically forcing herself to keep calm, she moved around the pony, frantically trying to work out how to save her friend.

Joanne's head and shoulders were clear of the pony, but her arms were pinned under him. Amber swooped down on her friend and shouted at her to wake up. Joanne didn't respond. Amber remembered from safety classes that she had to leave her where she was as she might have damaged her spine and it could be made worse by movement. On the other hand, if Joanne was left lying under Flash's immense weight, she could easily be crushed. Making a decision and hoping it was the right one, Amber bent down and put her hands under Joanne's shoulders. She grabbed her and pulled with all her might, but it wasn't enough. Joanne remained pinned.

She couldn't get Joanne out from under Flash and her actions had made things worse. The movement of pulling at Joanne had disturbed him.

At first it was just a gentle, testing movement, but then, as Flash realised he was caught in the wire, he started to thrash around, wildly trying to free himself. Knowing that he risked doing himself and Joanne a serious injury, Amber went to his head and tried to calm him down, but it was to no avail. Flash was in a blind panic and she could do nothing to appease him.

Hysteria threatened to take over. But then Pearl approached and rubbed her muzzle against Flash. His eyes rolled back to look at her and he stilled, though his chest was heaving and he was foaming at the mouth. Amber had never seen anything so shocking and upsetting.

She wracked her brains to think what she could do. She needed to get help, she had to find Elisha, and she had to keep Flash calm before the situation got even worse. She pushed her hand into her jacket pocket, searching frantically for her phone.

Nothing.

She checked the other pocket. "No, no, *no*," she wailed as an image of her phone lying on the back seat of the car pinged into her memory. Of all the days to forget to bring it with her!

Forcing her brain to think, she remembered that both Joanne and Elisha had their phones with them. She couldn't get at Joanne's, so she had to find Elisha and use her phone to get help. The next problem was how to go about it.

Amber knew that if she took Pearl away, Flash would be distraught, and he could tear himself badly on the wire if he continued to struggle. She knew she would have to go on foot.

With her mind made up, Amber put her plan into action immediately. Pearl was still close by, but to ensure she didn't wander off, Amber tied her reins to Flash's. She prayed that having Pearl with him would placate him until help arrived.

Amber placed a trembling hand on her pony's velvet soft nose. "Pearl, I need you to stay here and keep him calm. Can you do that for me?"

The pony stared intently into her eyes and Amber knew that she understood.

Amber hugged her tight. "I'll be back soon – I promise."

It seemed to work. Now that Flash knew that Pearl was close to him, he had quietened down. Feeling weighed down by her sodden jacket, she set off along the marked route to try and find Elisha.

As she followed the fence, all sorts of thoughts raced through her mind. *"Will I find Elisha? Is she safe? What's going to happen to Flash and Joanne?"* She couldn't believe all this was happening.

"Amber!"

She turned in all directions, sure that she had heard something.

"Amber, *help*."

This time she knew she had heard her name. She stopped and looked around but could see nothing through the rain.

"Where are you?" she called into the wind.

"Over *here*. Look right."

Amber turned and saw Elisha, bedraggled and ghostly white, crawling towards her. Without asking what had happened, she ran towards her and demanded her phone.

Elisha handed it over, all her self-assurance now gone. Amber dialled 999, her fingers trembling. "Ambulance please."

Elisha crumpled onto the floor crying and wailing, "Oh, what's happened? It's all my fault."

Amber described what had happened and where they were as best as she could from the sheet of very wet directions to the operator, while Elisha listened and snivelled even louder. Next, Amber phoned the police and told them there was a loose pony somewhere in the area and there had been an accident. Finally, she flicked through Elisha's contacts list and found her dad's number. She relayed the message to him quickly and hung up before he asked to speak to Elisha. She wanted to get back to Flash and Joanne as quickly as possible.

She positioned herself on Elisha's left side so that the injured girl could lean on her and take the weight off her injured right leg. As they hobbled back towards Joanne and the ponies, Amber found out that Elisha had been able to turn Rocky as they went careering over the top of the hill, but had been unable to stop him. They had gone some way at a mad gallop when she had grasped her right rein with both hands and proceeded to haul on it with the idea of turning the pony in circles of decreasing size until he slowed down and stopped. Unfortunately, Rocky had been going so fast that the sudden change of pressure on his mouth and the shift of his rider's weight had unbalanced him and he had fallen briefly. No harm had come to him and he got up immediately and galloped off into the distance, but as he stood up, he had stepped on

Elisha's right ankle. It was now extremely painful and she was convinced it was broken.

By the time Elisha told her part of the story, they had arrived back at the broken fence where Flash still lay, with Pearl standing beside him. The stricken chestnut pony seemed to be keeping his eye on her as she stood, for all the world acting like his guardian angel. As Pearl heard the girls' voices coming towards her, she turned her head and whinnied, glad Amber had returned, but not moving from her position.

When Elisha saw the horrific sight of the tangled, bleeding pony lying upon the unconscious Joanne, she fell to the floor, sobbing uncontrollably.

"This is all my fault!" she wailed, "if we hadn't been racing this would never have happened."

"But there was the jet," Amber found herself trying to ease Elisha's guilt.

"I know, but we were already going too fast. If I hadn't suggested that we race we would probably have been able to pull them up before they got to the top of the hill."

"Maybe," sighed Amber. She left Elisha weeping on the wet grass and went to stroke her pony.

As she rubbed Pearl's nose and buried her face in her pony's long, wet mane, she considered how lucky she was. She could have been lying at the bottom of this hill with a crushing weight suffocating her, or she could have a broken ankle and a missing pony. Instead, she had steadfast, sensible Pearl. And in that moment, Amber finally realised what it was that had always made her love Pearl so much: even though she wasn't perfect, Amber could trust her.

Cold as she was, Amber's whole body flushed again with shame at the times when she had envied Elisha and Joanne and their ponies, the times she had resented Pearl and wished she had a faster, more exciting pony.

"I'm sorry," she whispered into Pearl's ear, wrapping her arms around her neck. Pearl nuzzled her gently, silently offering her forgiveness.

Amber had never loved Pearl more than she did at that moment.

– Fourteen –

Good News

After what seemed like an age, a Land Rover rumbled over the top of the hill and bumped down to meet them. It had hardly stopped when Mrs Best, Mr Templeton, Mrs Jones and Mr Anderson flung the doors open and ran to their children.

Amber was enveloped in a tight hug from her father when she heard Mrs Jones' scream as she discovered her daughter trapped under the fallen pony.

"Joanne, oh God *Joanne!*" Mrs Best pulled the frantic mother away, telling her the ambulance was on its way and there was nothing she could do.

Elisha's dad ran to get a wire cutter from the back of the Land Rover, before leaning down to assess the damage. Flash's legs were covered in blood and parts of the wire had become embedded deep in the pony's skin as a result of his struggling. As soon as Elisha's dad attempted to remove the wire, Flash began to struggle again, his eyes widening in pain.

Mr Anderson rushed to help. He placed his hands on the pony's neck and gently stroked him. "Alright Flash, easy boy. We'll get you free."

Pearl, who had remained like a rock throughout the entire ordeal, placed her face close to Flash's. Their silent communication soothed the frightened pony. Flash placed his head back on the ground and lay still, breathing slowly.

Swearing quietly under his breath, Mr Templeton was able to slowly cut the wire before gently prising it away from the pony's legs.

The sound of sirens suddenly flooded the area and flashing lights appeared at the top of the hill. Seconds later paramedics were descending the steep slope carrying a stretcher and a large first-aid kit.

Working patiently, the two dads had managed to free Flash from the wire and were encouraging him to his feet.

He stood up shakily, a mass of blood and wide-open gashes, trembling furiously with pain and shock. Mrs Best produced an old blanket from the back of the car and threw it over him.

Now that they could gain access to Joanne, the paramedics examined her quickly. Without removing her riding hat, they fitted a neck brace and swiftly got her onto the stretcher, away up the hill and into the ambulance. Mrs Jones followed alongside, holding her daughter's hand.

As the sirens blared and the ambulance sped away, Mrs Best took charge. "Right," she bellowed, "Elisha can't walk, and she seems to be in shock. I'll take her to casualty."

"No," Elisha roared. "What about Rocky? I won't leave until I know he's safe."

"Right, Mr Templeton, you come with me. I'll drop you off at my house on the way to the hospital and you can start the search for Rocky."

Mr Templeton nodded at the woman's instructions and the three of them left in the Land Rover.

Amber, Mr Anderson, and the ponies were left alone in the rain. Suddenly realising how exhausted she was,

Amber began to sway against her dad. He helped her back into the saddle and tried to lead them back the way they had come. They only managed a few steps before it became clear that poor Flash couldn't be expected to walk anywhere with his injuries.

"It's not looking good Amber, I'll get your mother to bring the trailer," he said, taking out his phone and dialling first his wife's number, then the vet's office.

***

Joanne had been seriously injured. She had three broken ribs, a broken collarbone and wrist, a dislocated hip and significant muscle swelling from the overwhelming weight of the pony. The doctors said it was just as well the paramedics acted fast, or her injuries could have been life-threatening. Amber could not go and see her for two weeks as she was heavily concussed which made her very sick and confused.

After what seemed like years, the Andersons received a telephone call from Mrs Jones to say that her daughter was now up to seeing visitors, although she would have to stay in the hospital for some time yet.

Joanne was propped up in bed when Amber and her parents entered. She smiled at them and politely accepted the box of chocolates they had brought, but she looked very weak and fragile.

At first, Amber didn't know what to say to Joanne, who looked so awful and yet was being so brave about the situation. She also remembered how Joanne hadn't stuck-up for her against Elisha's taunts and wondered if they were still friends.

"How's Flash?" Amber managed to say after the pleasantries were over.

"Mum says he's pretty bad. He's cut into a tendon in one of his front legs and he's completely lame. The vet says he should come sound again but he might need at least a years' rest." She paused. "If he heals up ok and comes sound, we'll be selling him."

Amber was shocked at her matter of fact tone.

"Mum and Dad don't think he's safe for Matthew," Joanne said.

"Oh," mumbled Amber, unsure how Joanne felt about Flash being sold or whether he was safe for any child.

"But anyway," said Joanne, brightening up, "if it wasn't for you, Flash wouldn't be alive, and neither would I probably."

"What? What do you mean?" stuttered Amber in astonishment.

"Well, the vet said that if Flash hadn't lain as quietly as he did, he could easily have cut through an artery and bled to death, right there on top of me. I believe I've got you…and Pearl to thank for that."

Amber proudly remembered Pearl's untroubled steady assistance. Not only had she calmed Flash, but she'd also prevented Amber from panicking which had enabled her to compose herself and think clearly. She couldn't have done any of it without her wonderful pony's help.

"And the doctors said that if I had come into hospital much later, they might not have been able to save me. I had a lot of internal bleeding," she explained casually, "so if you hadn't got on to the ambulance so quickly…well… you know."

Amber sat in stunned silence, unable to believe what she was hearing. Joanne rambled on while Amber just sat and listened.

"Elisha broke her ankle. Just like her to get off lightly," she added testily. "The police found Rocky, heading right for the main road, thanks to you again, and he's absolutely fine, so I suppose all's well that ends well."

Amber couldn't believe she could be so positive about the accident when she could have been killed.

"No point dwelling on it I suppose," she thought.

***

Member's Cup was cancelled that year in light of the accident, and although Amber respected the decision, she was disappointed that people would not see Pearl's new and improved jumping ability.

"There's always next year," she mused, *"at least I know how wonderful Pearl is, even if nobody else does."*

The following morning, Amber sauntered wearily into the kitchen and saw a copy of the local newspaper on the table. She poured herself a glass of orange juice and pulled the paper towards her. Her eyes widened, and she slowly put her juice down before she spilled it. There on the front page was a picture of her and Pearl, taken at the farm earlier that year, under the main headline:

YOUNG GIRL'S BRAVERY SAVES FRIEND

The article chronicled all the events of the ride and the subsequent race against time to get help. The article finished with a quote that was taken from Amber's parents. *"When have they been speaking to journalists?"* she wondered.

> 'We are very proud of our daughter. She kept cool in a very difficult situation and did extremely well to raise the alarm as quickly as she did. We would like to add that our daughter's pony, Pearl, also played a vital role in the rescue operation and it couldn't have been done without both of them. They are both heroines.'

Amber read the article with her mouth hanging open. They had done it. Her wonderful parents had ensured she had got her wish. Now, not only did they know how special Pearl was; everybody would know.

Everybody.

Acknowledgements

I want to thank my parents for introducing me to the joy of books and stories. Some of my earliest memories involve bedtime stories, with *The Velveteen Rabbit*, *Peace at Last* and *The Troublesome Pig* being some of my favourites, followed by an introduction to fairy tales. Apparently, I knew every book off-by-heart and would tell my parents off if they tried to skip a page!

Mum and Dad have been with me every step of the way with the horses. I have been blessed to have two parents who shared my hobby, and my childhood was filled with hacking out and going to shows with them. Special mention to my dad who used to stay up after a night shift to take me to shows and who, now aged 70, still rides out with me, mucks out and drives me to competitions and training events. Thanks Dad, you're one in a million!

One of the hardest things about being a writer is having the belief in yourself that your work is good enough and that people will want to read it. Thanks must go to some of the early readers of the first version of *Little Pearl*: Sophie, Amber, Georgia and Maia, for their positive feedback, and to students I have taught who have unwittingly given me encouragement and confidence through their comments on my writing and ideas.

Thanks must also go to Amanda at Let's Get Booked, who designed the front cover, creating exactly what I wanted, and also edited the book, which helped to improve the delivery of the story itself and also ensured that the message I wanted to get across was clear. I wanted to show that in reality, the world of horse ownership and equestrian sport is often tough. You can go through blood, sweat and tears with them and still not get the result you'd like. Horses aren't machines, and to work with them you have to have a lot of patience and a willingness to persevere and accept your faults as a rider. I wish I'd known what I know now when I had Little Pearl. I wanted to put some of the lessons I've learnt into this book for the benefit of riders who are just starting out. Amanda really helped with her constructive comments and suggestions, and her input was invaluable in making the book exactly what I set out to create.

And finally, to my husband who had to put up with me being totally engrossed in writing and editing for months! Thank you for your support x

Glossary

Bit - A metal bar worn in the pony's mouth. It is attached to the bridle and reins and is used for directing and controlling the pony.

Camp - The members of a Pony Club branch spend a week with their ponies and receive instruction. They take part in competitions against each other and have fun while developing their horsemanship.

Cross-Country - A course of fixed natural fences, including hedges, ditches and water spread out over differing terrain and over a longer distance than show jumping.

D.C - Stands for District Commissioner- the person in charge of a Pony Club branch

Fell - a high and barren landscape feature, such as a mountain range or moor-covered hills. This book is set in Cumbria which is renowned for its landscape of fells.

Fly buck - A pony leaps forward into the air as if jumping over a non-existent obstacle.

Grackle – A noseband designed to stop the pony opening its mouth or crossing its jaw to evade the bit.

Hacking - A leisurely ride out.

Horse Trials - A competition comprising three phases: dressage, show jumping and cross-country.

Hunter Trials - A cross-country competition.

Martingale – A piece of tack involving a strap or pair of straps running from the noseband or reins to the girth of a horse, used to prevent the horse from raising its head too high.

Member's Cup - A branch competition where members of the same Pony Club compete against each other in age groups. The elements of the competition are: written test, turn out, equitation, dressage, show jumping, handy pony and games.

Pelham – A type of bit used for a strong horse to prevent them from pulling too hard.

Rein back - A dressage movement where a horse is asked to back up. The rider puts their leg on to ask for forward movement, but prevents this with the reins so the horse moves backwards. This is also a useful technique for opening gates while mounted.

Studs – Studs can be screwed into a horse's shoes to give them better grip. They can help prevent slipping and give the horses more confidence. There are different types of stud to use for different conditions e.g. hard ground or soft ground.

Tetrathlon - A competition comprising four elements: shooting, swimming, cross-country (riding) and running.

Turn on the forehand - A dressage movement that involves moving the horse's hindquarters around his front legs. This is another technique that is also useful to allow a rider to open a gate without having to dismount.

Two-point seat – When jumping and galloping, riders move into the two-point position which is a more forward, out-of-the-saddle position. This allows a horse to open up and move forward while rider ensures their weight is balanced on the horse.

Under-horsed - When someone rides a horse or pony that is too small for them or is below their capability as a rider.

Weaving - A pony sways from side to side, shifting its weight from one foot to the other while it looks over a stable door. It is a vice (bad habit) and is usually due to boredom, frustration or stress.

About the Author

Helen has been horse mad all her life. Her adventures with ponies began back in 1990 with Little Pearl, but they are still continuing now with her three horses, Maddy, Charlie and Holly who are all just as interesting and individual as Pearl was.

Maddy is the first horse Helen bought for herself, using money given to her for her 21st birthday. Maddy is quite like Pearl: full of personality and mischief. She has got herself into more trouble over the years than all the rest of the horses put together. Maddy enjoyed Riding Club activities for many years and has done everything from British Eventing to Pony Club games. She's a real fun horse who is now semi-retired, but still enjoys hacking out.

Then there's Charlie, AKA the Ginger Tank who thinks he's a thoroughbred racehorse but was sadly born into the body of a draft horse. He loves jumping, beach rides and charging about on cross-country courses.

Finally, there's Holly, the sensitive girl who is a sweet swot – always wanting to get things right – with an anxious side. Helen is still working on ways to get the best out of her as she has a lot to give but worries too much, completely unlike Maddy and Charlie who couldn't care less and just take life in their stride!

When Helen isn't busy writing books or playing with horses, she is also a secondary school librarian and English teacher. Just as well, as the loves of her life are reading, writing and riding!

She lives in Cumbria with her husband, horses and a variety of dogs, hens, ducks and geese!

Visit www.helenharaldsen.co.uk to find out more about Helen, her books and her horses.

You can also sign up to the mailing list to receive news, competitions and opportunities liked to Helen's books, as well as free bonus *Amber's Pony Tales* content– available exclusively to subscribers.

Did you enjoy this book? The author would love to see your reviews on Amazon.

Please feel free to post your comments and let others know about Little Pearl.

Look out for THE SECOND BEST PONY – the next book in the series.

Printed in Great Britain
by Amazon

51093206R00080